Where is the Apple Pie?

written and illustrated by **Valeri Gorbachev**

Philomel Books • New York

To Patti

Patricia Lee Gauch, Editor

Philomel Books, a division of Penguin Putnam Books for Young Readers,

345 Hudson Street, New York, NY 10014. Philomel Books, Reg. U.S. Pat. & Tm. Off.

Published simultaneously in Canada. Printed in Hong Kong by South China Printing Co. (1988) Ltd.

Book design by Marikka Tamura and Patrick Collins. The text is set in Worcester Round Medium.

The art for this book was completed with pen-and-ink and watercolors.

Library of Congress Cataloging-in-Publication Data

Gorbachev, Valeri. Where is the Apple Pie? / Valeri Gorbachev.

Summary: A simple question leads to the description

of a more and more outlandish situation, but never really gives an answer.

[1. Animals—Fiction. 2. Questions and answers.] I. Title.

PZ7.G6475Wh   1999   [E]—dc21   98-35695   CIP   AC   ISBN 0-399-23385-7

1 3 5 7 9 10 8 6 4 2

First Impression

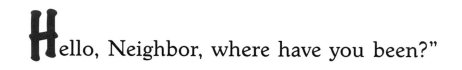

Hello, Neighbor, where have you been?"

"To the bakery."

"What did you buy?"

"An apple pie."

"Where is this apple pie?"

"Robbers took it away."

"Where are the robbers?"

"They ran into the forest."

"Where is the forest?"

"The fire burned it down."

"Where is the fire?"

"The water put it out."

"Where is the water?"

"It ran into the lake."

"Where is the lake?"

"The camel drank it up."

"Where is the camel?"

"In the desert."

"Where is the desert?"

"Beyond the horizon."

"Where is the horizon?"

"Covered by fog."

"Where is the fog?"

"The wind cleared it away."

"Where is the wind?"

"Blowing right down Main Street!"

"Blowing right down Main Street?
Where you bought the apple pie
that the robbers took to the forest
that the fire burned down,
where the water drenched the fire,
and the lake drank the water,
and the camel drank the lake
and disappeared into the desert
just beyond the horizon
all covered with fog,
until the wind came along
blowing right past the bakery
where you bought the apple pie?
That Main Street?"

"So where is the apple pie?"